To Debbie

panay Roberto kangul allilla llanca puito sonco.

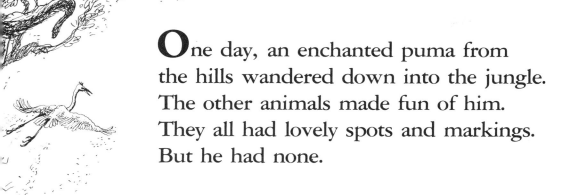

One day, an enchanted puma from
the hills wandered down into the jungle.
The other animals made fun of him.
They all had lovely spots and markings.
But he had none.

The puma left.
He traveled for days.
At the top of the mountains
he saw a tree with a condor nest.

As he snatched an egg to eat it,
Father Condor appeared.
He pounced on him.
"I will break you in pieces," he said.

Up, up, up he flew.
When he was very high up,
he dropped the puma.

Puma went tumbling down.
Sticks, stones,
change my bones,
he said, uttering magic words
to save himself.

Puma was at once changed into a log.
And he landed at the edge of the cliff.

Lucas the water carrier, was coming up the road.

Lucas had a hole in his fence.
He had been looking for just such a log, to fill it.

Lucas took the log home and stuck it in his fence.

Puma waited for night to come.
When everyone was asleep,
he repeated the magic words, saying,
    Sticks, stones,
    change my bones,
and turned himself back
into a puma again.

He ate all the chickens
and in the morning, changed
himself back into a log again.

When the farmers
found their chickens missing,
they were furious.
"I will make a trap
to catch the thief,"
said Lucas.

He went to the waterfall for reeds.
As he cut them down, he heard a croaking.
"Help me. I am caught under a stone,"
called a frog.
Lucas ran to free the frog.

"Lucas," the frog said.
"The log in your fence is no log.
He is an enchanted puma.
He changes himself into a puma at night
and eats all the chickens. I have seen it."

"So!" Lucas said. "If that is how it is,
then I know what to do."

Lucas went back home.
He heated water in a caldron, as if
he were making a soup.
When the water was boiling, he seized the log
and threw it into the water.

"Aii-ee!" Puma cried. Quickly he said,
>*Sticks, stones,*
>*change my bones,*

changing himself into a puma again.
And he leapt out of the pot.
The boiling water had turned his fur to gold.
And the flames had left their mark.
He ran to the jungle.

The other animals gathered around him
to admire his golden color
and his beautiful spots.
And, because he looked so different,
they gave him a new name – *otorongo.*

That is the story they tell in Peru
about how the plain puma
got his spots and became the
beautiful otorongo of the Amazon jungle.

The Animals in the Book

Tree porcupine

Giant anteater

Cebus monkey

Piraña

Puma

Wolf

Armadillo

Tamandua

Caimán

White-face monkey

Toucan

Kinkajou

Great white heron

Agouti

Tapir

Coati

St. Lucia parrot

Green lizard

Giant tortoise

Maguari stork

Capybara

Paca

Three-toed sloth

Sparrow

Land iguana